The Fanatics

Dedication

I dedicate this book to my pastor, Eric T. Pittman, who held a Prophecy Conference at Hope Baptist Church. During this conference, Dr. Tom Sooter took a portion of time to expound on the probable future of Christianity in America. This conference sparked the idea for this book, which I hope you find as enjoyable to read as I found it to write.

Chapter 1

"Breaking news," blared the radio reporter excitedly. "Just in: The *2018 Hate Crimes Bill* has just been amended again. It is now illegal and punishable by death to believe and press those beliefs on anyone else, including your children, that there is only one true Bible, that there is an afterlife or only one way to reach it, that there is only one true and right religion, that there is only one God, or that any certain thing allowable by law is a 'sin'. The authorities in our government have termed these people as menaces to society and dangerous to our children's delicate psyches. They have also stated that these people are murderers, causing nearly every suicide there has been in this country, due to their imposing false guilt upon the children of America. This Bill was followed up by an announcement just minutes ago that anyone reporting the whereabouts of these, what the government is terming, 'Fanatics' to the law will be handsomely rewarded. The number to call if you wish to report a 'Fanatic' is 1-555-2Report; that's 1-555-273-7678."

Lydia coiled at the announcement like she had just been belted across her delicate chin. What would they ever do? She gazed at her three small children as the panic began to rise within her chest. They had to teach them about Jesus, there was no way around it. Her children would not go to Hell because of a law. No, she would not, could not, allow that, but… surely God did not expect them to give their lives to tell other people about the Gospel… and only God knows what would happen to the children if they were caught!

Lydia glanced toward her husband, realizing that he had been thoughtfully studying her worried countenance. She would not even have to tell him what had been running through her head. He was very observant. He would know exactly what she had been thinking.

She loved staring into Clyde's emerald green eyes. She always found the confidence there that she lacked. How could he always have such solid faith in every circumstance? Even with the dreadful announcement they had just heard, he still had a peace about him that was beyond her comprehension. The faith *her* man held in the Heavenly Father was absolutely remarkable! That is the thing she had always loved most about him… his wonderful, unshakable faith in God. Oh how she wished she could have just a little bit of the faith he had, but it seems there is always a worrier in every family, and in this family, she was the prime candidate.

She looked down at her hands, folded neatly in her lap. "We're not going to stop telling others about Jesus… are we?" she asked, already knowing his answer.

"No," he answered slowly, shaking his head. She loved the way his red hair captured the light. He often told her that her long, curly, black hair captured the light as well, sometimes making it appear blue.

"No," he said again. "How can we stop obeying God? Christ gave His life for us. How can we do any less for Him?" He paused briefly to ponder his words, as was his custom. He rubbed his chin with a work calloused hand in a nervous gesture, as if he were trying to rub off some of his many freckles. "If it is God's will to keep us safe from harm, then He will, but if He wills that we be martyrs for Him, we must count it a privilege and honor to have served Him as He sees fit." He looked deep into Lydia's blue eyes. "I love you, Lydia."

"I love you too, Clyde. I just pray that I can be as strong as you if and when that time comes."

"I have faith in you, Dear. Have faith in yourself... More importantly, have faith in God."

"Sometimes, Clyde, you are remarkable. I don't know how you do it. I'll try. God will have to do the rest. Oftentimes, faith is a big word that is much easier said than done."

"I know, Dear. I know." They united in a long, endearing embrace.

Clyde knew he had to be strong for his wife, but deep inside he was uncertain as well. He too hoped God would help him be strong if the worst was to happen. Growing up in a home where his parents drank and cussed incessantly, he had no knowledge of Christ or His sacrifice on Calvary until he was twenty-three years old. A small group of men had come to the jail, where he was being held for violating yet another law, to preach to the inmates. When he decided to sit in on a service just for something to do, he had no idea the effect it would have in his life. He had never heard of this man called Jesus. He could not comprehend a selfless love, for all he had known was hate, but Jesus accepted him just as he was when he saw himself as a worthless sinner and begged God's forgiveness so he could be free from a devil's Hell. From that day forward, he was a changed man. He was hungry for anything about God that he could get his hands on. He grew very quickly in the things of God and never stopped growing. That was fifteen years ago, and he was still going strong on the unshakable foundation of Jesus Christ. What a great God he serves!

*   *   *

Clyde shot straight up in bed. Yes, there it was again, an unmistakable pounding at the door. Who could that be… and at this time of night? He peered again at the clock to be sure he had read it right the first time. Yes, 3:30 am. He crawled groggily out of bed. "Just a minute, I'm coming," he yelled, throwing caution to the wind. If the pounding on the door had not awakened the children, then they would sleep through anything! As he opened the door, Lydia peeked around the corner.

"Who is it, Honey," she asked wearily. Clyde did not reply, nor did he have to, for an armored S.W.A.T. team followed by uniformed police officers were forcing their way into the living room. Clyde tried to run toward the back of the house to protect his wife and children, but was stopped by a bullet in his back. Lydia jumped back and rushed towards the children's room. She had to get to her precious children; they must be terrified! She did not get far, however, before she was wrestled to the floor and handcuffed.

Grace, the oldest of the three children, had the other two huddled with her in a dark corner. They had all heard the pounding on the door and were immediately awakened. They were all making their way toward their bedroom door to satisfy their curiosity when they heard the outside door bang open, and lots of people, including their daddy, shouting. By the time the gun was fired, they were all already hiding. Grace tried to keep her sister and brother quiet so they would not be found, but they were both crying uncontrollably, after all, they were only two and a half and four years old.

"I'll be back," she said, rubbing their heads.

"No," they cried. "Don't leave us!"

"I have to. I have to get help," she whispered. "Just stay here and be quiet and you'll be okay. I'll be back, I promise." She quietly slipped away from their death grips and crawled out the bedroom window. She did not even look back as she sprinted into the woods. She did not know where she was going. She had no idea. All she knew was that she had to find help… fast. God would lead her to the right person. God would take care of everything. He had to. After all, He loved her, didn't He? Tears began to spill down Grace's face. She did not want to cry, she had to have a clear head, had to see where she was going, but she could not stop. The further she ran, the harder she cried. Did God love her? How could He love her and her family and still allow them to suffer? Then she remembered a verse Daddy had drilled into all their heads over and over again, "And we know that all things work together for good to them that love God, to them who are the called according to *His* purpose." No, it was not God's fault. Yes, He allowed it, but He had a purpose. It would be okay; yet, she could not stop crying.

Chapter 2

21 years later

The large crowd stirred restlessly. Things were not going very well. They had spent countless hours battling the "Fanatics", and to no avail. The small group seemed to grow despite the opposition. It was almost like the opposition they were providing to this sect was *making* them grow, like it was *fertilizing* their movement! ...But how could that be so? Something more *had* to be done... and soon! This could not go on any longer.

It was Bob Parker's turn to speak. He approached the podium with confidence and ease, his large body swaying back and forth as he walked in his usual nonchalant pace. His manner seemed to help everyone else relax a little bit. "The Fanatics are growing more and more violent," Bob said. "Be weary of your surroundings. Do not allow yourself to be caught alone. They are everywhere… waiting for a chance to strike." Bob Parker paused, sensing the temperature of the crowd. "In fact, one our own men, Jonathon Zoner, was attacked by a group of them last night while on patrol duty." A gasp swept across the crowd. Bob Parker held up his hand in comfort. "Not to worry," he stated matter-of-factly. "Jonathon is just fine. In fact, he is here tonight to tell us exactly what happened."

Jonathon Zoner approached the podium quietly. It was evident to most in the crowd that he was nervous, but who wouldn't be? His long, lanky legs allowed him to take long strides to the platform. His bushy black hair bounced on top of his head with every step. He soon reached his destination behind the wooden podium. It completely shielded his skinny body from view where Bob Parker's had protruded in many directions just seconds before. Jonathon, or Jon, as many affectionately called him, gripped the top of the podium with such fervency that his knuckles began to turn white. He stared nervously at his hands. "Lord, please help me," he prayed silently to himself. Then he looked boldly at the crowd and began to tell his story.

"Last night, around 11:30 pm, I rounded a corner on my patrol shift to find an older man, probably in his sixties, accompanied by a beautiful young lady around twenty-six or twenty-seven years old." A snicker passed through the crowd as they saw Jon blush at his admission of attraction to this unknown woman. "At first, I was startled, as they came up on me so suddenly, but I believe they were just as surprised to meet someone around the corner as I was." Jon paused to contemplate his next words.

"Is that when they attacked you?" Someone asked too loudly. A murmur swept over the crowd.

"I wasn't *attacked* per se, just confronted. They asked me a very simple question. 'If you were to die this very instant, where would you spend eternity?'"

"So they *did* threaten you, then!" Another person spoke out blatantly.

"No," Jon said. "They did not threaten me. When they asked me the question, I could tell they really cared about my soul. They told me how Jesus died on the cross because we are all sinners and cannot get to Heaven on our own. Then they told me that all I have to do is believe that Jesus is God and that He died and arose from the dead, and I can go to Heaven. I was in no way attacked." Jon smiled shyly as he finished. He turned to walk away from the platform.

Everyone sat in shocked silence. "He's one of them," someone whispered from somewhere in the middle of the crowd.

"He's one of them!" someone else yelled out for all to hear. "Get him! Don't let him leave! He's a Fanatic too!" With that, everyone rushed toward Jon, but he escaped through the back door and across a field into the darkness. One of the uniformed police officers shot his firearm into the darkness, but it was too late. The fugitive had escaped.

"It's too dark to find him tonight," Bob Parker said, "especially with all these woods around. Let's all go home and get a good night sleep. We'll track him down in the morning. With any luck, he'll think that we gave up, and his trail will lead us right to the others." Everyone agreed to the plan, and then everyone except Bob separated toward their homes. He had to stay at the compound for a few moments longer to finish a few things up.

After walking back inside the building, he finally found himself alone. Now he could think about what he had to do next. This was no easy thing. Thoughts whirled around inside his mind like a tornado had been let loose in his brain. This assignment would not be as easy as just tracking down any other Fanatic. This would be different, but what else could he do? He had to detach himself from his feelings. Somehow he had to forget the impossible and focus on the job at hand. Yes, he was angry about the occurrence. Very angry, but Jon was... He couldn't let anyone else know how he felt. He had to hide it... to masquerade... his re-election hinged on him being strong. If he faltered in this, he knew any chance of him being re-elected in two months was out the window. He had to figure this out, to focus.

"Why didn't you do something?" The voice came from the front row of metal fold-up chairs in the room where the meeting had just taken place. He knew that voice. It was his granddaughter, Kellie.

"What are you talking about, Dear?" He asked.

"You know what I am talking about, Grandpa. Why didn't you stop them from trying to hurt Jon? You are the Police Chief. You could have stopped them. Instead, you encouraged it. You encouraged a hunting party for tomorrow… for him to be hunted down, like a common… *animal*."

"He's one of them, Kellie. He's a Fanatic. You know the law. It's my job to uphold the law."

"But he's your grandson!" she yelled in frustration. "He's my only brother! You could have stopped it!"

Bob tightened his jaw. "He's no relation of mine. I refuse to be known as the grandfather of a *defector*. I am

American—born and bred. And if you know what's good for you, you will disown him too. He's nothing but trouble now that he is one of *them*."

Kellie defiantly stood to her full height of five foot 4½ inches. "He is my brother, the only person in my family I have left besides you," she spat out. "I am not going to give up on him... not this easy."

"Kellie, after you join them, there is no turning back! It's a life of exile or imprisonment! You choose to be loyal either to your brother or your country. Jon is a fugitive now. Do what's right!" Bob was trying to talk some sense into the beautiful blond haired, blue-eyed girl, but he knew that she was going to be stubborn, just like always.

"I am doing what is right," she said defiantly, "with or without your help," then she spun on her heel and marched away from her grandfather... probably forever.

Chapter 3

The long prayer meeting was about to draw to a close. The small group of Baptist believers had met—just like always—in the small church building on Pastor Jack Sander's property. His home was out in the middle of nowhere, miles from civilization, and would be difficult for government officials to find. He had known from studying the prophecy in the Scriptures that hard times were coming for Christians, and he had dutifully bought two thousand acres of property under the false name of John Matthews and had secretly built a small community in the very center of the heavily wooded acreage with the help of a few carefully chosen individuals. They had wisely dug a deep well, bought farm animals such as chickens for their eggs, goats for the milk, horses, and beef cattle. They had also stock-piled food, guns, ammunition, clothing, garden tools, plenty of seeds for two year's worth of home-grown food that would reproduce with the replanting of dried seeds, and other essentials. This was to be a safe haven for those who loved God and sought for the much-needed protection from the laws of the land.

Pastor Sanders was slowly walking to the pulpit, his worn King James Bible in his hand, as was normal for him. His very presence demanded attention and awe from his parish. This had nothing to do with his height of six foot two or his broad muscular shoulders from years of working hard on "The Haven of Rest" as he affectionately named his property. Instead, this deep respect for the man of God stemmed from the fact that he was the very reason that many of his parishioners were still free to live out their lives in peace… at least for the time being.

"For most, it is a very scary world we live in. Our rights have been stripped from us one by one. First they took our right to pray or mention the name of God in the schools, then they stripped us of our right to bear arms, then it became a crime to preach against Sodomy and fornication as the good old King James demands of us," Pastor Sanders waved his beloved Bible in the air to emphasize the point. "The Bible says we are not to shun to declare all the counsel of God in Acts 20:27. Then they tried to bar us from witnessing and telling others of Christ, labeling it harassment. Now, it is illegal to be a Christian at all. True, we have a safe haven to live in, a safe place for our children to be, but we must not stop obeying the Word of God. We must continue to tell others of Christ! God commanded us to go into all the world and preach the Gospel. His command does not become null and void just because the law says it's illegal! Acts 5:29 says, 'We ought to obey God rather than men.' Do be careful. Pray about whom to approach. God will lead you to the right people. The most important thing any of us can do right now is to pray, and the right prayer is always, 'Thy will be done'."

At that very moment, the back door on the little church house burst open, causing everyone within to startle, and some to scream out in alarm. In stumbled a very scared looking man, completely exhausted and out of breathe. Everyone stared at this tall man in fear as they took in the facts. He stood about six foot tall and was almost too skinny. He was about twenty-five years old, had a deep complexion, deep-set blue eyes, and a thick bushel of black hair on top of his head. The fearful part was that he wore a gray police uniform.

No one moved. What were they to do? They had been found. Their beloved "Haven of Rest" had been given up. Someone had turned them in, and now they would all suffer the consequences. Pastor Sanders stepped confidently toward the man. He walked up to him like he was walking up to an old friend. He reached out a helping arm to the young man before him; he was going to help him to a chair so he could get his breath when the young man suddenly collapsed into his arms. Many wondered why Pastor Sanders was being nice to this police officer, the person who could, and probably would, take the freedom from each and every person there... why he seemed to have no fear of the situation. As they wondered on this matter, Pastor Sander's daughter, Grace, stepped out from her seat and rushed to help her father care for the young man. She promptly noticed everyone staring at her and quickly, to everyone else's shame, quoted Romans 13:9, "Thou shalt love thy neighbour as thyself."

She helped her father lay the man onto the floor and removed her hand from behind his back. Her hand was covered with blood. She carefully rolled him onto his side to examine the wound as her nursing training had taught her to do. The round, deep wound was low and to the right side. It appeared to be a bullet wound. Maybe an arrest went wrong? The bullet could have pierced his kidney, but it was hard to tell what direction the bullet took since there was no exit wound. She would have to wait until she got him onto a cleaner surface to examine the wound more carefully. She felt inadequate to care for this man, but the extensive training she had received from Doctor Betty would have to suffice. The "Haven of Rest" had been very fortunate many times to have had a medical doctor living among them, but now the task had been passed on to Grace since the old woman had passed into Glory not too long ago.

"I think he's been shot," Grace said.

"We should take him into town, close to the hospital, where someone can find him and care for him properly," someone said.

"We can't do that!" someone else amended. "He got here once, he can get here again… and next time he'll bring reinforcements."

"We can't exactly keep him here against his will," said Pastor Sanders, "but we can't turn him out into the streets hoping someone will find him in time either. He could die. He's wounded pretty badly. I need someone to help take him to my house. We'll figure out what else to do after he is feeling better."

Chapter 4

Jonathon Zoner had no idea where he was or how he had gotten there. All he knew was that he was tucked securely inside a warm bed. The last thing he remembered was running frantically through the woods… running for his life. He knew the reception, or lack thereof, which he had received from the people at the town meeting, was a possible reaction, and a probable one, but he wanted so badly to share the Jesus he had met with his dearest friends. He wanted them to have the same chance he had, the chance to feel the overwhelming peace that knowing Christ brought, the true love that He surrounded you in, and the undeniable knowledge that no matter what you did, Heaven was your home. He had hoped beyond all hope that they would listen, that they would understand the urgency of the message, for Jesus was coming soon, that without Him they would all be left behind to face the terrors of the Tribulation Period with absolutely no chance of Heaven! ... His family: Grandpa Bob and his sister, Kellie... he had to get back to them. He had to make them understand! Without Christ they were doomed to an eternity in Hell!

As he lifted his right arm to throw back the heavy handmade quilt that covered him so he might crawl out of bed, he was instantly met with an intense pain that shot through his back like lightening. He breathed in sharply as it took his breath away. He groaned quietly in protest. Even the sharp intake of air hurt! He lay back down on the bed as slowly as he could as he tried his best to relieve the pain.

"I thought you would never wake up", a singsong voice in the corner called out sweetly.

Jon turned to see the lady who spoke... *too fast, that hurt*. He winced in pain. The young lady had stood and was placing the book that she had been reading in the seat of the rocking chair she had been occupying. She turned and slowly began to walk toward him, looking almost scared. Who was this beautiful girl with her long black hair, short, skinny figure, and pale complexion? She moved so gracefully that she almost floated above the ground. None of this mattered. He had to get back to his family. He had to tell them what he had learned about Christ.

"Where am I," he asked, still enchanted by her mere presence, though he wished himself to focus on the matter at hand.

She looked down at the floor, then back up at her patient. "How are you feeling? You gave us quite a scare."

"Where am I?" he ventured again. Maybe she didn't hear him.

"Here, let me check your wound. I got the bullet out. It wasn't as deep as I thought it would be. You must have been almost out of range of the gun."

Was that curiosity he heard in her voice? Was it curiosity about him? Surely he could trust her with the truth. No, he could not trust anyone... even if they were as beautiful as... as an angel.

She helped him roll onto his side, and then she unwrapped the bandage to look closely at the wound. "Looking good," she reported giddily. "In about two weeks you should be as good as new."

"Two weeks?!" he cut her off. "But you don't understand! I have to get back home. I have to tell them what I learned. I have to tell them about…" He decided it was better to leave the sentence unfinished. If these people, good though they were, knew that he was what most called a "Fanatic", he was sure to leave there in a police car… if he left there alive.

She looked at him quizzically for only a moment. Then, she continued, "You should stay still as possible for the next few days, then it wouldn't be a bad idea for you to start moving around a little… but just a little." She carefully applied more medicated salve to the area and re-bandaged it. "Be sure to get lots of rest. I'll bring you something to eat in a few minutes." With that, she turned and hurried away, probably to telephone police headquarters to notify them of his condition and location… wherever that was. He had to get out of there. If they called headquarters, no matter how innocent it was, he would be dead by morning, no doubt about it. The trials for Fanatics, if there was one, lasted all of five minutes, always found the defendant guilty, and always ended in death. He had not left anyone reason to wonder about his stand on the issue the last time he had addressed the city council. He would probably just be shot on the spot.

Sighing heavily, he tried to relax himself a little. Maybe then some of the stiffness he felt in his muscles would subside. He looked slowly around the small bedroom that held him captive. It was bright with shiny white walls that were interrupted only by two windows and a large picture of a sunset over the ocean. There were two other strategically placed small pictures to accompany it, one of jumping dolphins, and the other of a sailboat on a peaceful bay. The long sky blue curtains hung in loose folds. They were swept back from the windows and held with a matching wide piece of cloth. Jon noticed that the room did not have a light fixture in the ceiling or a lamp on the bed stand. There was no clock on the wall or on the dresser. He did notice an old oil lamp and some used candles. He thought it was odd, but let the thought quickly pass as the clean windows let in plenty of natural light.

Jon did not feel much like eating when the young lady had returned with a plate full of vegetable lasagna. His stomach was in knots. He had been looking for his clothes when she had casually returned with the food. He had managed to get himself out of bed only to find out that all he was wearing was green and white plaid pajama bottoms that belonged to someone in the household, no doubt the lady's husband.

"What do you think you are doing out of that bed?" she asked.

"Looking for my clothes," he offered. "I have to get back home."

"I'm sure you do. And you *can* leave… as soon as your back is healed enough for you to make it there safely." She set the plate of food on the bed stand and walked to his side to help him back into bed. He didn't like that he had to rely on her so much for support as he walked, but it was a necessity. She helped him into bed, propped some pillows so he could comfortably sit up and eat… or at least as comfortably as he could with a hole in his back… and handed him his plate of food.

"I'm not really hungry," he said looking down at the lasagna.

"Nonsense. You haven't eaten anything in at least twenty-four hours. That's how long you have been here. You have to at least try to eat."

"Where exactly *is* here?" he asked setting the plate in his lap.

"Your food's getting cold," she retorted.

"Tell you what, you tell me your name, and I'll try to eat." Jon said.

"My name?" she looked a bit frightened. "Names don't matter. What matters is that you get the proper nutrition and rest so you can go on fighting crime like a good little cop. Now eat up." She smiled at him, the sweetest, most pleasant smile he had ever seen. "Go on, try a bite. I promise you'll like it."

Hesitantly, he lifted his fork to his mouth. It was good; in fact, it was beyond good, it was delicious. But he still wasn't sure if it would stay put. His stomach lurched in response, then, surprisingly, it quieted down and gratefully accepted the rest of the homemade meal.

Chapter 5

As Kellie carefully picked her way through the dark woods, she was thankful for what light there was from the half-grown moon overhead. She did take the time to go to her small blue sports car for the flashlight that she always kept in the glove box, but she quickly noted with quiet frustration that the batteries were near dead, offering little or no help in the way of seeing where she was going. She dared not make too much noise when she passed the building that held her grandfather inside. She did not think that he would hurt her, but she was not quite sure anymore. If he were not willing to stand up for his only grandson, would he stand up for her? Would his precious career be more important to him than she was? It was certainly more important than Jon! How could he? She slapped back a small tree branch in anger. It swung back, slapping her in the face. *Oh! That would leave a welt!* "Just my luck," she thought.

Stopping short, she realized that she had not been paying attention to Jon's trail. Where had it gone? She could not have lost it that far back. She had just stopped paying attention a few short moments ago. She would have to stop all this bellyaching and focus on the task at hand. Besides, complaining never helped anyone… Of course, it never hurt either. But then, there was the old adage… "A blonde cannot do two things at once". *Dope! Yep, proven true again… looking for the trail. Okay, here we go. Gotcha, Jon.* Then a thought hit her like a box of rocks. If she could follow him so easily… in the dark, how long would it take a group of blood thirsty men to track him down in the light? She had to do something.

Looking back over the path from which she had come, she knew that no small task lay ahead of her. There were broken twigs, trampled ground, and many spots where Jon's blood had wiped onto tree branches and leaves. How would she ever cover his tracks? It was going to be a long night! No, maybe covering his tracks was not the right answer. There was no way she would be able to revive the ground and twigs and get all the blood cleaned up... especially in the dark. No, maybe she should make a few other paths, pull them off Jon's trail. But how? Blood is hard to replicate without bleeding, and she had a phobia of bleeding to put it mildly. Then, when the trails led nowhere, they would eventually come back to Jon's true trail and find him! What would she do? She could never save her brother... not by herself... not unless she could find him first and get him safely hidden. It might help too if the clear sky miraculously filled with clouds and a pounding rain washed all trace of him away... after *she* found him, of course. With *that* settled, she started on her way again. It would soon be midnight. She only had six or seven more hours before the hunting party took to the woods, then all hope would be lost.

She walked all night long. Around two-thirty in the morning, it did start raining. Not the hard, pounding rain she had hoped for, but a slow steady drizzle was better than nothing, and who knew? Maybe it would just work! Although the turn in the weather would make it harder for Jon... and herself... to be found, she had a hard time not being down about it. The ever-soaking ground made her footing less sure. Now, on top of the raised welt on her face, which her hand kept self-consciously touching, she was soaked to the bone and covered with mud and leaves. She was sure there were twigs in her hair and maybe a bug or two as well. Yep, Jon would certainly get a laugh when he saw her... if she could ever find him.

Around six-fifteen, things started to look up a little. It had finally stopped raining, the sun was peeking out from behind the horizon, and it was not as scary being in the woods alone anymore. Kellie still did not relish the idea of the "alone" part, for she was a people person. If there was a crowd, you would find her in it. She could not stand being in solitude, but for her brother, she would do anything, even walk alone in the muddy, dripping woods. "Jon, you had better be thankful, but not too thankful. You *are* going to pay for this!" she muttered to herself. Running her hands through her wet, tangled hair, she hoped she would find him soon so she could cuddle down into a nice bathtub full of hot water and peaches and cream scented bubbles... those were the best as far she was concerned.

Mmm, peaches and cream. She was hungry! Her stomach grumbled in protest to the lack of nourishment. She had never thought of *eating* peaches with cream before, but it did sound good... especially right now. She had not thought of grabbing any food from her car. She always kept supplies in the trunk in case she got stuck in the snow or something. But then again, that would have been a lot to carry. Yep, Jon was definitely going to pay... later. Right now, she *had* to find a well-hidden place to bed down. She was so bone weary she could barely pick up her feet. If she did not get some sleep, she would fall over from exhaustion. She figured she had at least ten hours head start on the posse. If she only slept for two or three hours, that would give her plenty of energy to find her brother, and she would still have a great head start. Looking around, she saw a large fallen oak tree nestled down into some heavy underbrush. Only the top of the trunk was sticking out. That would do just fine. "Sweet dreams, here I come."

Chapter 6

Jon tossed and turned all night long. He dreamt many things, but one dream was not new. This dream had been haunting him for a few months now. He, Kellie, and a faceless girl were all in a room together. They were huddled in a kind of scared group. He wasn't sure why they were scared or why the two girls were trembling so, but he could tell that something was definitely wrong. It was dark. He could not see very far, but he knew he was in a bedroom, maybe in a closet? He could hear voices in the distance. They were angry voices. They were yelling. There was a gunshot that was so close it vibrated his body. He always woke up in a cold sweat at that point, sitting straight up in bed with a gasp. Yes, tonight had been no different… except for one thing. Tonight, the third person had a face. It was the face of the young lady who had been caring for him so vigilantly since he arrived at… wherever he was.

But why would she be in his dream? Why did she seem so very familiar? Why did he feel a connection to her, like they were meant to be together forever? He did not feel attracted to her like a man is normally attracted to a girl. True, she was beautiful, but it was something deeper. It was almost like he knew her… from somewhere. It was like they had had a deep relationship at one time… a relationship he could not remember. He knew it sounded silly, but he *had* to find out *who* this woman was and why she stirred up all these emotions inside him. Maybe this *was* what it was like to fall in love? He had never been in love before. He had never had time. He had always devoted his life to the police force. Grandpa Bob had big things planned for him, and he had to work hard if he was going to attain them. But, maybe…

"Snap out of it, Jon Boy! You can't do this to yourself. You have more important fish to fry. I can't think about myself right now, I need to get to Grandpa Bob and Kellie. I have to tell them about Jesus. Besides... she wouldn't have me if she knew I was a... a "Fanatic". Not only that, but I could never put any woman in the position of losing the man she loves." And lose him she would, for he meant to tell Grandpa Bob and Kellie about Christ. That in and of itself was a death sentence. No, he could never subject anyone to that. And...to be married to a "Fanatic", even if you were not one yourself, could mean a lot of trouble too. "I have to get out of here... fast," he thought to himself. He knew if he did not leave soon, not only might he get caught and lose any chance to save his family, but he might also lose his mind!

Slowly, he crawled out of the soft bed and inched toward the chair where he knew his pants had been neatly folded and placed. He was told that his shirts had been thrown away. They could not get the blood out of them, and the hole, he was told, was not mendable. He cringed as he reached for his pants. He was feeling a little better, but it still hurt so bad to move. Slowly, he donned his clothes. He decided to keep the shirt on that he had been loaned. He was much too modest to walk around half clothed. Slowly he sat down at the small, sturdy oak desk in the far corner of the room. There was a small pad of stationary paper and a blue ballpoint pen in the top drawer. He hated to write on the pink paper, the arrangement of red roses in the top right hand corner of the paper and the fallen petals lining the bottom of the paper definitely gave it a feminine touch, but he had no other choice. Normally he would have just scrawled a quick "Thank you" on a notepad, but he had to tell them. Besides, he'd be long gone before they found it. This way they would learn the Gospel too. He hoped he could remember what to say.

I'm sorry I don't know who to address this to, since I did not learn your name, but thank you for your hospitality. The food was great too. I'm sure you'll be none too pleased to learn you helped a Fanatic, but I must tell you about Jesus. You see, He died on the cross for you, to take your place, so you don't have to go to Hell. Everyone was headed for Hell because we are all sinners. We all do bad things. But, God looked down at us and knew He had to do something for us because He loves us so much. He sent His only Son, Jesus Christ, to earth to be born of a virgin and live a sinless life, which only He can do since He is God. He then allowed wicked men to crucify Him, but it wasn't only their fault that Jesus was put on that cross. It was our fault too. Your and my sin put Him on that cross.

His love for you and me held Him there. He died there for us. He was placed in a tomb, and then three days later He came back to life! He can do that, because He is God! If you believe that you do bad things, any of which will send you to Hell, believe Jesus died and rose again so you can go to Heaven, and ask Him to take you there, you can go to Heaven too. Won't you please accept Him? Just pray, "Dear God, I know I am a sinner. I know You died for me. I know You rose again. I cannot get to Heaven without You. Please save me and take me to Heaven when I die. In Jesus name, A-men." I hope you decide to believe on Jesus. If not,

do not bother to look for
me. I am long gone.

God Bless,
Jonathon Zoner

Chapter 7

"Finally," Kellie said to herself, "people!" She saw a scant pillar of smoke off in the distance and headed toward it. "Maybe they have seen Jon." Slowly she made her way through yet more briars. Would it ever end? When this was all done and over with, she would be happy if she never saw or heard about another tree for the rest of her life! Even during her nap, she dreamt about trees! "Nap... whoever heard of a seven hour nap!" she huffed. She had slept *a lot* longer than she planned on. When she woke up and saw that the sun had already started its downward descent in the sky, she panicked, but not for long. She quickly realized that with the long rain last night it would be near impossible for anyone to find her, never mind Jon. She *did* feel rested, but she was still hungry. That had not gone away. "I guess sleep doesn't cure everything," she thought.

"Jon better appreciate what I am doing for him," she growled. "I must be a mess by now." She looked down at herself in disgust. Her long black dress pants and new red satin blouse were covered with dirt. Her normal peaches and cream scent was gone, and in its place was a smell of... ugh, she did not dare go there. She had not forgotten that her hair was a rat's nest of leaves and sticks, and to top it all off, she was sure she *still* had that welt and maybe even a black eye! Who knew, these people might just laugh at her and send her on thinking she had escaped from the looney bin or something! As she emerged from the woods, she heard a beautiful voice singing, but she could not quite make out the words. The tune sounded somewhat familiar, but she could not place where she had heard it before. The singing woman was busy hanging clothes on a line, unaware that anyone was watching her.

As Kellie drew closer, she could hear the words more plainly, " 'Twas grace that taught my heart to fear, and grace my fear relieved. How precious did that grace appear the hour I first believed."

"Oh, great," thought Kellie sarcastically. "Fanatics. If Jon did stumble on these people, at least he'll be with his own kind." She did not exactly think they were animals like Grandpa Bob did, but she definitely was prejudice.

"How can you be so happy when all you know has been ripped away from you, and you have to run for your life?" she quipped toward the singing girl, whose back was turned toward her.

Grace froze. The plain yellow dress she was about to hang on the clothesline fell forgotten to the thick grassy floor of her backyard. So, they HAD been found. Their worst fears had come to realization, and yet, somehow, there was a strange peace. Grace slowly turned around to face the mob of police officers that were undoubtedly behind her to find an all too familiar face. Grace had dreamt of her face every night since that dreadful day so many years ago. True, Kellie was much older now, but she had not really changed that much, and... she looked just like Momma. Grace hesitantly took a small step forward. "Kellie," she breathed in a faint whisper. "Oh, Kellie."

Kellie stared back at her, almost too scared to move. Who was this small figure of a person who stood before her? How did she know her name? Why did this woman's presence affect her the way it did, giving her an odd sense of comfort and warmth? Who was this woman? Kellie stumbled backwards, tripping over a small boy behind her and falling awkwardly to the ground. Almost immediately, people were there to help her to her feet. She felt lightheaded and faint. She had not had anything to eat for so many hours—yes, that must be it; she was faint from hunger. Still, something about this lady before her was *too* familiar, almost frightening. Kellie took in a slow, deep breath to slow her heart and to get her wild imagination under control. When she trusted herself to speak, she said, "Look lady, I don't know who you are or who you think I am..." Kellie stopped short as the woman reached out her hand to gently trace her jaw line with her long index finger.

"Kellie, it's me," the woman said lovingly. "I'm your sister, Grace."

Kellie could feel all the color drain from her face. "No," she whispered, "it's not true." She backed away in shocked disbelief. "I don't know who you are or what kind of sick joke you *think* you are playing... my sister died almost 22 years ago..."

"But, Kellie, it *is* me. Remember you always called me 'Rae-rae'. You started when you were just learning to talk and it stuck. I called you 'Kells'. Then there was Jonny-boy."

Jonny-boy? Kellie had not heard that name in years! *Rae-rae? Kells? How could this woman know all this? It could not be... And yet...* Kellie's world started to spin. She tried to stay on her feet, but it was futile.

The next thing she remembered she was lying on the soft grass with the warm sun beating down on her tired body. The cool washcloth on her forehead felt good. *Where was she? That's right. Grace was telling her... Grace!* Kellie sat up so fast she nearly fainted again.

"Easy there, Sis," came the sweet voice she had been conversing with earlier, the voice of Grace... her sister.

"But how... how did you... everyone thought you were dead." Kellie choked out the words as she tried to hold back a torrent of tears. She secretly cried over the loss of her sister, her best friend, at least once a week. Grandfather would never approve of such childlike behavior. "We had a memorial service. We couldn't find you. We looked for three weeks. They said you didn't survive the woods, that no five year old could ever survive the woods alone... not for that long." Kellie slowly looked around her at the small group of concerned people who had gathered around her. "... But then... you weren't alone... were you." It was more of a statement of awe than a question, but Grace felt it needed, deserved, an answer.

"Poppa, Jack Sanders, was out hunting when he found me stumbling through the woods. I was crying so hard I could barely see. I walked right into his back, scared him to death. He said he nearly used the bathroom on himself," she said with a chuckle. Wiping a tear from her cheek, she looked up toward the bright blue sky as she pondered how good God was to lead her to that very spot. If she had not literally bumped into Jack that day, she may have died, pure and simple. "He took me in as his own. I didn't talk for months after it all happened," she said quietly, shaking her head. Finally he was able to drag the story out of me, piece by piece, until he had all the facts about that horrible day." She sighed deeply, and then continued, "I have lived here ever since."

Kellie stared at her with an empty stare. *What was she talking about? It? Horrible day? What scared her so badly that she would not utter so much as a syllable for months?* "Grace? What *are* you talking about? Did Mom and Dad's arrest really scare you *that* badly? They *were* defectors. Besides, Grandpa said they'll probably get out soon. They are very close to renouncing, you know. He said they have finally decided that keeping up this Jesus nonsense was not worth their freedom. Well, I say it's about time," she spat in anger. "I think they have definitely kept us waiting long enough. Didn't care very much about us to let us grow up without them, did they?"

Kellie looked up at Grace to see tears fill her eyes and spill down her pale cheeks again. Did she not know the truth? Grace turned and ran toward the nearest farmhouse. Kellie sighed deeply and dropped her head in shame. Of course she did not know. She had been here for twenty-one years. How would she know? She had probably made up her own fantasy about Mom and Dad, one that ended more in her favor... who could blame her? Now, Kellie had found her sister and scared her off— emotionally anyway, in one day. What a great day it turned out to be. Just perfect.

Kellie heard quick footsteps padding the ground as they came closer to her... probably Grace's husband coming to shoo her away. She looked up, knowingly, but was taken aback when it was Grace herself, peering down at her with pity. In her trembling hand she held a yellowing newspaper. Slowly, gently, she handed it to Kellie. She looked down at the page that was folded back, "September 22, 2020." That was the date it all had happened, so Grace did know the truth, she just refused to accept it. But… why would she bring a newspaper that proved what Kellie had to say? She read the headline,

"FANATICS CAPTURED…

Late last night, the Tennessee State Police received a tip from Police Sergeant Bob Parker concerning the whereabouts of yet another family of what the force has termed *Fanatics*. 'This dangerous sect must be stopped at all costs,' stated Parker. He certainly lives what he teaches, as last night's Fanatics were his own son-in-law and daughter, Clyde and Lydia Zoner."

No, that could not be true. Grandpa Bob loved her and Jon. Why would he turn their parents in? He always said it was a shame they had been

turned in at all, that he believed children needed their parents. He said that he was sorry for them, that he was angry with the person who separated their family! And it had been him all along? Kellie read on:

"Clyde Zoner offered resistance at the arrest, attempting to aid in the escape of other guilty parties and necessitated deadly force to be stopped." *Deadly force?* "His wife, Lydia Zoner, will be tried Monday, September 25. If found guilty, she will face execution the following day." *Execution!* "Two of their three children, Jonathon, 2 ½ years old, and Kellie, 4 years old, have been placed with their grandfather, Bob Parker. The third child, Grace Zoner, 5 ½ years old, has run off into the woods and has not yet been located.

Police Sergeant Bob Parker stated that he is sure the search will turn up little Grace by tomorrow evening."

Kellie dropped the paper into her lap. It suddenly felt so heavy she could not lift it. Could this be true? Had Grandpa been lying to her all this time? Had he caused the death of her dear family? Had he been the cause of all the unspeakable grief she had suffered? Yes, it had to be true. The papers did not lie. Suddenly she was filled with so much hate she thought she might explode. She would kill him! She would kill him if it were the last thing she did!

Chapter 8

Grace was glad one of the other ladies had offered to care for the mysterious stranger in police clothes today. If she had to check in on him every few minutes and cook his meals too, she would not have gotten her house work done early, and she would not have had any time to spend with her dear sister. "Praise God! He knows everything in advance. He knows how the day is going to go. He knows what needs done so it all falls into place. What a great God we serve!" Still, she should probably check in on the man. She felt embarrassed that she did not know his name, but she was not willing to offer hers and felt it would be an unfair exchange to ask for his. Besides, he had never offered his name either. Strange.

She would ask Kellie if she wanted to go see him with her. She hated missing spending any more time with her sister than she had to. *Her sister*. That had a nice sound to it.

What was it that she had come for anyway? She had seemed so alone and lost. She was quite a sight too, covered in dirt, damp clothes, and a red face. Did she even say? No, but it did not matter anymore. Kellie had come to her. The two sisters were united! She would have to ask her about Jon. How was he? Grace knew he had undoubtedly grown up a lot. She probably would not recognize him if she bumped into him in the street. No, he was only two years old when she saw him last. And was he ever cute! He had pudgy, pink cheeks, bright blue eyes, a head full of bushy black hair, and antics to beat the band. Yes, he was quite the character! Some of the things he would say and do in pure innocence would send any sane person into fits of "roll on the floor" laughter. Such a cutie. Grace sighed in reminiscence. Those were the days, and that was what she missed the most about not being with her sister and brother as they grew up… seeing them grow up. She had missed them so very much. They had a lot of catching up to do! Grace hoped Kellie would live with them, that she would not return home… wherever that was. She had missed out on so much with her already. Surely she felt the same way. But then, there was that unmistakable hatred that had filled her eyes when she had read the newspaper clipping. Something about that scared Grace. She had not known Kellie since she was four years old. That small, innocent, loving child could have changed so much in that time. She *had* changed. The Kellie she knew did not know anything of hate. She could not remember Kellie ever getting saved, and that is what scared Grace the most. Momma had never pushed that on any of her children. She wanted them to come to the realization of needing a Savior on their own so they would not have any doubts in the future. If Kellie were still unsaved, which her prior words and actions had suggested, that would certainly account for the unmasked hatred seen in her eyes. Grace had to find out about her sister's soul. She had to witness to her… even at the risk of running her off. She could not bear anyone going to Hell for eternity, and definitely not her very own Kellie. She *had* to tell her… now. Of course, maybe seeing the injured man could be a good jumping board for telling Kellie about Jesus. Yes, that would be great! Grace hurried to finish carefully tucking the aged newspaper clipping into her black chest in her bedroom and rushed downstairs to where Kellie waited for her on the front porch of her Poppa's house.

Kellie sat perched on the very edge of the porch swing. She was biting her lip, and her brow was furrowed in deep thought. She looked kind of cute like that, but Grace needed to break the reverie. "So, can a nosy sister know what it is that you are thinking so hard about?"

Kellie jumped. "Oh, sorry," she said, "I didn't hear you coming. You startled me a bit."

"So…" Grace dug, "What's the big secret?"

"I'm looking for my brother… our brother," she caught herself and looked up in apology.

Grace's dainty mouth fell open a little as she crinkled her brow and shook her head in unbelief. Surely she had not heard her sister right. She did not know where their brother was? The newspaper clipping said they were both placed with Bob Parker. Surely he would not be cold hearted enough to separate the two siblings... or would he?

Quickly noting Grace's response, Kellie hurried to explain, "He announced to the world in a town meeting dealing with the rise of Fana..." Kellie looked up apologetically.

"Fanatics. It's okay. You can say it," Grace laughed. She knew that was what they were called and she expected no less from Kellie since she *was* part of that world.

"I'm sorry," she stumbled. "It's just that... out *there*," she made a sweeping motion with her hand, "*that* is considered an insult."

"Well, not here. We are honored to be known to go all out for our God." Grace's eyes showed that she meant every word she said.

Kellie cleared her throat, took a deep breath, and continued. "He told everyone that he's, uh, one of you kind of people, and they are after him. They shot at him when he ran out the door, and I think…" she paused to clear her throat again. It was tight with anxiety. "…I think they got him." She started to cry then, deep, heart-rending sobs. "And… I don't… I don't know if… if he's… okay…" She buried her head in her hands and rocked herself back and forth as she had done so many times to self-soothe. Grandpa Bob said she gave in to her emotions much too easily, but he just did not understand. How could he? How could anyone that had never been through as much as she had? Now, to think that she might have lost her brother, that he might be out there dying… or dead, was too much to bear. What would she ever do without him? He had been her entire life since she was forced to grow up so quickly so many years ago. Grandpa Bob provided food and shelter for them, but there was no emotional support, no bond. She had to provide that to Jon even when she felt so empty inside herself, and at four years old, that is a lot to ask! She felt she had every right to cry now. He was her everything!

She had not even noticed that Grace had moved to kneel in front of her. Placing a tender hand on her head, she softly tried to caress away all the hurt, but there was so much. Only Jesus could ever heal this much hurt. Only Jesus can heal anyone. "Kellie, honey. I know right now you feel like no one cares. You feel like no one understands, but there *is* Someone Who knows *and* understands *everything* you are going through, everything you have ever gone through."

Kellie did not look up, but she *did* listen, basking in the comforting voice of her sister.

"God's *only* Son, Jesus, was wrongfully murdered right before His eyes. He knew it was going to happen before He even created this world, before He made you and me. He knew that we, even though He made us perfect and innocent, would sin, that we would choose to disobey God. He knew that He would have to provide a perfect Sacrifice to make a way for the people that He loved so much to be able to be united with Him again in the sweet communion He craved. He knew that man's sin *had* to be punished in Hell's eternal fire, and

He *knew* the ONLY way of escape for His beloved creation was the death of His only begotten Son, Jesus Christ. Jesus came to Earth through a virgin birth, lived a sinless life, as only He can do because He is God, and offered Himself a sacrifice for sin. The men He created condemned Him to death, beat Him so badly you could no longer tell He was even a man, nailed Him to a rugged cross, and watched Him die as they gambled for His clothes. They hated Him *so* much, but, hanging up there on that cross, He *still* loved them... loved us. He even prayed that God, His Father, would forgive them for the awful thing they were doing. He will too, if we accept the gift He offers us of salvation. He came back to life three days later, Kellie. He could. He is God. Now He is standing at His Father's side watching you every day. He is hoping right now that you will choose to believe on Him, that you will choose life. Kellie, please. This is so important."

Kellie did look up now. She could hear the earnest pleading in her sister's voice. There were tears in her eyes. She really did care for her like she said. She really did believe it was as important as she said.

"But it's so scary... How can you choose to give everything up for something that you're not even sure is true?" Before she even said it, Kellie knew she had made a mistake. Grace *did* believe it, with all of her being. She could see it in her eyes, in her face. She almost had a glow about her. But... *how* could she be so sure?

"I do know, Kells. But even if I didn't, I would much rather believe now than take a chance later and find myself in Hell. And as to how I can be willing to give up everything for Him... with all that He did for me, how can I offer Him anything less than my all?"

Kellie still had a lot of uncertainty within her. Everything she knew and every ounce of common sense screamed at her to run away. She knew what happened to defectors, to Fanatics. She had seen it first-hand. Her Grandpa Bob had brought hunting parties to their home more than once to refuel and go again. She had begged to be part of it, to be out there in the action, but he always said someone needed to stay home and keep the home fires burning. She had longed to be out there helping to murder innocent people simply because they believed in God. She had even turned someone in once. But what if it was true? Would so many people willingly give their lives for something that was false? She had never really thought about it before, but it did not seem possible. These people whole-heartedly believed what they preached. But if it were true, would God even accept her? How could anyone, especially God, love her? She had done such terrible things. How could He ever forgive her?

"Does He forgive everyone?" Kellie was stunned to hear herself asking. "Does He save *everyone* from this... Hell?"

"Yes," Grace breathed in a sigh of joyous relief. She knew in her heart of hearts that Kellie was about to receive the gift of life. "Yes. He will receive *anyone*. You can never be too bad for God to forgive. The price He paid on the cross was sufficient to pay for the sin of even the most vile and wicked person who ever lived. All you have to do is ask." Grace held her breath as she waited for her sister's response. It seemed like forever.

Kellie looked up at her through her tears. She had to do it. She *had* to. She felt a shoving, a tugging, at her heart. She could almost see Jesus just as Grace described Him hanging on the cross. She could hear Him say, "Father, forgive them." She knew she was included. She shook her head yes, slowly at first, then quicker and with more force. If these people could live in exile, running for their lives, and still *want* what it was that Jesus offered, she wanted it too. She had seen the joy and peace that filled these people. She saw the happiness. She did not understand it, but she wanted it. "Yes. Tell me how."

Grace started crying then. She was so happy. She shook her head right along with her sisters. Yes, she wanted Jesus! "Kellie, have you ever done anything wrong?"

A look of astonishment came across Kellie's face. If she only knew... She shook her head in affirmation.

"Good, because God can only save you if you are a sinner to begin with." Grace smiled so big Kellie thought her face might disappear. She wished she would get on with it. She did not want to wait a moment longer. She was scared the ground would open up and she would fall into Hell right now if she did not hurry. She *had* to hurry! "You do know that the penalty for sin is Hell."

"Yes."

"Jesus died on the cross to pay for that sin. He died so you don't have to go to Hell."

"I know."

Grace loved to see a sinner at the edge of salvation. The determination and conviction on their faces alone was enough to give her energy to last a month of Sundays without food or water. She could always tell when they were close. That this particular sinner was her own sister, the sister she had prayed for so many times, was almost too much to bear. "Jesus said, 'That if thou shalt confess with thy mouth the Lord Jesus, and shalt believe in thine heart that God hath raised him from the dead, thou shalt be saved. For with the heart man believeth unto righteousness; and with the mouth confession is made unto salvation.' If you believe that Jesus,

God's Son, was born of a virgin, died and rose again three days later to pay for *your* sin, just tell Him."

Kellie's head shot up to look into Grace's eyes. "Tell Him?" The perplexed look in her eyes was enough of a question without the actual words to accompany it.

"Talk to God in prayer, just like you are talking to me right now."

Kellie looked hard and deep into Grace's eyes. Talk to Him like they were talking now? That sounded easy enough. "God," she began. She did not know what to say, so she just poured out her heart. "I'm really sorry I caused Your death on the cross because of all the bad things I do." She paused to sigh deep. "You knew I was going to sin before You made me, yet You did it anyway, You love me in spite of it. I'll never understand it all even though I want to. I believe You died for me so I won't go to Hell, and I am telling You that now. Please save me from Hell." Kellie looked up in relief. She felt so much lighter, like a heavy burden had been lifted from her shoulders. Somehow, she felt at peace. It *was* real... no doubt about it. It was real!

Throwing herself into her sister's embrace, they cried on each other's shoulders. God was so good.

*　　*　　*

"Oh! I almost forgot what I came down to ask you," Grace said a few minutes later. "I'm on my way upstairs to check on an officer that found his way here the other day, and I thought you might like to tag along."

Kellie shot straight to attention, "An officer! A police officer? Was he wearing his uniform? Was he shot? What's his name?"

Kellie talked so fast Grace had a hard time sifting through her words, but finally realization hit her. Jon had been shot at a town meeting. "Is Jon an officer?"

"Yes, yes. Is that the man's name? Is it Jon?" Kellie did not wait for an answer. She excitedly bolted in the front door and up the stairs. Somewhere up there was her baby brother! She had no idea which room to look in first, and thankfully Grace was right there beside her, pointing her in the right direction.

Grace opened the door containing the mystery guest and stood aside so Kellie could enter. She almost knocked her over in an attempt to hurry inside to see her brother... only he was not there. Grace saw the hope drain out of Kellie's face. She saw the expectation vanish, but the hurt did not return. Jesus had taken that away.

"Where is he?" she asked.

Walking over to the desk in the corner, Grace investigated what she thought to be a hand written note and found it to be so. She read Jon's letter, first to herself, then out loud. "It was Jon!" she said excitedly. "It was our brother! He never told us his name, but look, he signed the note, right here. It says 'Jonathon Zoner!'"

Kellie continued to stare at the floor. "But where is he now? He's out there all alone... hurt."

"We'll find him Kellie," Grace said rushing to embrace her sister. "We'll find him."

Chapter 9

Jon had been traveling for what seemed like hours. After days... he did not know how many days he was there... of eating so well, his stomach demanded food every few hours. And... he had been hungry now for about two hours. He was beginning to feel faint. He slowly lowered himself onto a fallen log. He told himself that he was still as strong as he used to be, that he could go on for days without eating. He told himself he was sitting down simply to assess his situation. After all, he had to make sure he was heading the right way. He should have brought food, but he could not exactly just ask for it, "Excuse me, I'm sneaking out of here tomorrow morning. Could you bring me some extra sandwiches? And, wrap them if you could." Jon chuckled at his own joke, but quickly caught himself as the sudden movement made him wince in pain.

Jon felt badly about leaving the way he did. He wished that he could have given them something in return for their generosity, but what did they need that he could give? Other than the need of salvation, these people seemed to have everything covered, and he had left them a letter explaining that in detail. Had he told them thank you? He could not remember. Surely he did. He tried to remember what he had written. Had he explained everything right? What if he did not remember to tell them everything they needed to know to go to Heaven? What if he forgot something? What if these people went to Hell because he forgot an important detail? It would be all his fault! He could not clearly remember what he had written. He had been so uncomfortable. His back was still hurting so badly.

As he was thinking over the letter, his "nurse's" face quickly took over his thoughts. She had been beautiful. Why *was* she so familiar? He wished he could remember. Did he know her from somewhere? Then he remembered... he remembered being on patrol, walking around a corner, and finding an older man and a girl, no, a young woman there. That was the night he got saved. It had been so dark, and they had stood in the shadows, but he was pretty sure... It had to be. He remembered her build, her long hair, and her voice. That voice could not be forgotten! The young woman and his "nurse" were one in the same! He did not know if the old man was there or not. He had not seen anyone else during his stay at that house. But, yes! She was definitely the same girl. That meant... she was a Fanatic too! That meant... she would accept him! Did she feel the strange connection too?

No. He could not think like this. He *had* to tell his sister and Grandpa Bob about Jesus, and he knew what that meant... imprisonment and execution. Rising slowly from his seat, he checked the location of the sun in the sky and started once again on his journey. He would not have gotten as far as he had if it had not been for the abandoned walking stick he had found near the edge of the woods. It was simply a rough stick with a smooth rounded top, but it was sturdy for leaning on, and for that he was thankful. He *had* to keep moving despite the pain that movement caused. He *had* to get to his family before it was too late. That was the last thing he remembered before collapsing on the wet ground from the pain and slipping off into oblivion.

Chapter 10

"Over here, Sir", shouted the tired officer. They had been hunting for Jonathon Zoner for almost three days now. Police Chief Bob Parker was relentless. He told everyone to keep searching. "He could not have gotten far," he said, "He's shot for goodness sake. How far could've *you* gotten like that?" He tried hard to keep everyone's morale high by offering rewards as they broadened their search for the escaped "Fanatic". Many wondered if it was worth it. "Besides", they murmured, "we could've captured three or four families of Fanatics in the time we've spent searching for Jon alone!" Everyone was tired and getting into a bad mood. They were all ready to go home, but someone *finally* found something.

"Over here," he repeated excitedly. "I've got something!"

Everyone stared in disbelief as Bob Parker ambled over to the man. "What did you find, Son?" he asked in his matter of fact tone.

"Right here, Sir," he said, "It's a piece of a gray uniform!"

"Great job. Keep up the good work." With that, the Police Chief turned and walked away.

Was that all he was going to say? ...After all the hard work ...all the excitement? Did he not see what this meant? They were finally on his trail!

"Listen up, everyone," it was the Police Chief speaking. "We have found a clue to his trail at long last. We have found a piece of torn uniform. There are no footprints in the vicinity of the fabric. I know it rained a few days ago, but there should be some slight impressions close by. I want everyone to be careful where you step. Look for brown blood spots, footprints, more fabric, anything that will give any clue to the direction he took. Let's get going, and good luck."

With that, everyone looked to their left and right to be sure they were still in a straight-line formation that was suitable for sweeping the terrain and continued on in their slow pace. Everyone's spirits had suddenly lifted. They were on the right track. They were finally headed the right direction.

It was not long before someone came across something else of interest, a dropped police issued firearm. Another officer found a footprint. They were getting closer! They would find him soon; of that there was no doubt.

Chapter 11

"Rock of Ages, Cleft for me, let me hide myself in Thee", the congregation finished the familiar song and were seated. Everyone seemed to be in high spirits tonight. They all sang loudly and boldly.

Pastor Jack Sanders took his place behind his pulpit to begin the Wednesday night Bible Study. Looking down at his notes, he looked back out at the congregation. Tonight was going to start kind of different. He was not sure how it was going to be received. None of that mattered. He had to preach what God laid on his heart. He was planning on preaching on the Blessed Hope of the Christian, the Rapture. That would be no problem, but the way he was going to present it might cause some hard feelings. *Here it goes...*

"I was thumbing through a book the other day when I came across an interesting story of antiquity. It tells of a band of soldiers, known as the "Emperor's Wrestlers", who served the Roman Emperor Nero:

"Fine, stalwart men they were, picked from the best and the bravest of the land, recruited from the great athletes of the Roman amphitheater.

"In the great amphitheater they upheld the arms of the emperor against all challengers. Before each contest they stood before the emperor's throne. Then through the courts of Rome rang the cry: 'We, the wrestlers, wrestling for thee, O Emperor, to win for thee the victory and from thee, the victor's crown.'

"When the great Roman army was sent to fight in far-away Gaul, no soldiers were braver or more loyal than this band of wrestlers led by their centurion, Vespasian. But news had reached Nero that many Roman soldiers had accepted the Christian faith. Therefore, this decree was dispatched to the centurion Vespasian: 'If there be any among your soldiers who cling to the faith of the Christian, they must die!'

"The decree was received in the dead of winter. The soldiers were camped on the shore of a frozen inland lake. It was with sinking heart that Vespasian, the centurion, read the emperor's message.

"Vespasian called the soldiers together and asked the question: 'Are there any among you who cling to the faith of the Christian? If so, let him step forward!' Forty wrestlers instantly stepped forward two paces, respectfully saluted, and stood at attention. Vespasian paused. He had not expected so many, nor such select ones. 'Until sundown I shall await your answer,' said Vespasian. Sundown came. Again the question was asked. Again forty wrestlers stepped forward.

"Vespasian pleaded with them long and earnestly without prevailing upon a single man to deny his Lord. Finally he said, 'The decree of the emperor must be obeyed, but I am not willing that your comrades should shed your blood. I am going to order that you march out upon the lake of ice, and I shall leave you to the mercy of the elements.'

"The forty wrestlers were stripped and then,

falling into columns of four, marched toward the center of the lake of ice. As they marched they broke into the chant of the arena: 'Forty wrestlers, wrestling for Thee, O Christ, to win for Thee the victory and from Thee, the victor's crown!' Through the long hours of the night Vespasian stood by his campfire and watched. As he waited through the long night, there came to him fainter and fainter the wrestlers' song.

"As morning drew near one figure, overcome by exposure, crept quietly toward the fire; in the extremity of his suffering, he had renounced his Lord. Faintly but clearly from the darkness came this song: "Thirty-nine wrestlers, wrestling for Thee, O Christ, to win for Thee the victory and from Thee, the victor's crown!'

"Vespasian looked at the figure drawing close to the fire. Perhaps he saw eternal light shining there toward the center of the lake. Who can say? But off came his helmet and clothing, and he sprang upon the ice, crying, 'Forty wrestlers, wrestling for Thee, O Christ, to win for Thee the victory and from Thee, the victor's crown!' "

He paused and peered at the congregation. So far... so good. He had everyone's attention. He continued. "We had a Vespasian here among us not too long ago. In fact, he just left sometime today. You may know whom I am talking about: a tall, skinny fellow wearing a police uniform. This young man, whom we now know as Jonathon Zoner, used to be a police officer, fighting on the side of the law to track down Fanatics and capture them for the sake of imprisonment and execution. When he stumbled upon our Haven of Rest, he must have been running from that same law. He must have been, for both the bullet in his back and the letter he left for Grace when he departed declare this to be so. To the shame of everyone here, no one witnessed to this man. No one cared for his soul. No one told him of Christ, yet in his letter, he witnessed to us. He told us of a saving Jesus. He told us of the death of God's Son, His resurrection, and His power to save if we will only believe.

"I understand the untimely entrance of a police officer scared many of us, but isn't it still our job to go into ALL the world and preach the Gospel to EVERY creature? Peter and the other apostles were placed in prison for preaching Christ in Acts chapter five. They were set free by an angel and told to go into the temple and preach Christ again. They obeyed and were again brought before the council, which consisted of the Sadducees and the High Priest. These demanded of them, in Acts 5:28-29, 'Saying, Did not we straitly command you that ye should not teach in this name? and, behold, ye have filled Jerusalem with your doctrine, and intend to bring this man's blood upon us. Then

Peter and the other apostles answered and said, We ought to obey God rather than men.' Then Peter told the council about Christ and His saving power. The council then took the apostles and beat them, and the apostles went away rejoicing that they were counted worthy to suffer shame for the name of Christ! Acts 5:42 says, 'And daily in the temple, and in every house, they ceased not to teach and preach Jesus Christ.'

"Should we do any less? Those who die without Christ are headed to a devil's Hell! The LORD is coming soon to take the saved away, and those without Christ will face the Tribulation Period, then Hell as well! There is a judgment day coming for the Lost where they will stand before the great White Throne Judgment and face the wrath of God Almighty. How can we do any less than witness of the saving power of our LORD and Saviour Jesus Christ? II Corinthians 5:11 says, 'Knowing therefore the terror of the LORD, we persuade men.' We MUST tell others about Jesus! We must!

"Jesus is coming soon to take us all to Heaven with Him. It will happen in an instant, in the twinkling of an eye. The Bible says we will all be here going about our normal business one moment, and the next moment, we will disappear. We will be caught up with Christ in the air to be forever with the LORD. Those who are left behind, those who do not believe on Christ, will be sent a strong delusion. Even if they knew about the rapture coming, they will not believe it. Those who have heard of Christ before will never have another chance to accept Christ again. They will be doomed to Hell. We must tell them before it is too late! We must tell EVERY creature about Christ. We must make them understand. They must know about the Saviour before it is too late. Let's Pray."

Chapter 12

The tired officers finally stopped for dinner before continuing their search of the woods. "Ham sandwiches and chips *again*," mumbled the officer who had found the torn piece of Jon's uniform. He shoved it into his mouth ungratefully. "I will be so happy when this rat race is finally over."

His companion peered at him quizzically out from under gray bushy eyebrows. "I'm just glad they're feeding us," said the old man. The combination of his bald head, bushy eyebrows, and three days growth of stubble made him look so comical that the first officer almost lost his bite of sandwich in a fit of laughter.

"I don't see what's so funny," the old man said. He shot up from his seat on the soft pine needle covered forest floor, grabbed his gear, and turned to stomp off in a huff.

"Where are you going, Patrick?" Police Chief Bob insisted in a low growl.

"Gotta relieve myself, Sir," he lied and continued on his way. He had not walked far from the group when he noticed a queer heap by a tree. "What on earth?" he wondered aloud. Moving on cautiously towards the heap, he noticed it was a uniformed officer apparently taking a snooze. Patrick chuckled to himself as he thought of all the practical jokes he could, and would, play on the sleeping comrade. Stealthily tiptoeing closer, he reached for a long stick to poke the man with. It was then that he noticed what he could not see before, hidden as it was by the odd way the man had been laying. This was not just *any* officer, for this officer wore a blue and white plaid pajama shirt. Quickly, he whipped his firearm out of the holster, aiming it at the unconscious man. "I've got something over here," he yelled. "I've got the Jon man himself!"

Everyone rushed over, tripping over each other, in an attempt to see the man who had for so long eluded their posse. Looking up at the sky in a thankful gesture, Patrick noticed a puff of smoke in the sky not too far away. Could it have been his eyes? Nope, there it was again. Pointing it out to the sheriff, he continued to stare at the strange occurrence. No one lived out in that area. But someone *had* to be there. More Fanatics? "It should be investigated, Sir."

"I agree," said the Sheriff and Police Chief in unison.

"Patrick, stay here with Jon," ordered the Sheriff. "He's out cold. Shouldn't be any trouble. The rest of you, follow me."

Moving on slowly toward the smoke, they were all soon close enough to hear voices raised in unison as they sang the dismissing song of the Wednesday Evening service. "This should be a cinch," chuckled Bob Parker to himself, "and with this capture, that re-election is for sure!" Motioning to the officers behind him to follow quietly, they quickly surrounded the building, pistols drawn.

"We have you surrounded," Police Chief Bob called out. "Come out slowly one at a time with your hands up, and no one will get hurt."

The singing inside stopped abruptly. There was a murmur followed by people shuffling about. Then, there was silence again. A young child began to cry from somewhere inside. "We're coming," said a strong voice from inside. "We're coming. We have our children with us. Just don't shoot."

Pastor Jack Sanders emerged first, followed by Grace. Kellie was the next person to walk out the door.

"Grandpa!" she shouted as she rushed towards him. "Grandpa, you don't know what you're..." A shot rang out that silenced the last word. Everyone stood dead still.

Bob Parker rushed forward to cradle Kellie in his arms. *NO! How had it come to this? Who fired that gun?* "Who fired that gun?" he demanded out loud.

"I'm sorry, Sir," the scared voice of a rookie officer whispered from beside him. "I thought..." his words dropped off as he watched his police chief gently stroking the hair of the young girl that lay so lifeless in his arms.

The sheriff quickly took over rounding everyone else up and herding them like animals into a large group. Turning to Bob Parker to inquire as to the next move, the sheriff was suddenly stopped in his tracks. Where had Bob's granddaughter gone? Bob still sat on the ground, his clothes were covered in blood, his hands were poised like he was still holding her body, but she was gone. Turning toward the large group of Fanatics, he was dumbfounded to see they had also somehow "disappeared". Where could they have all gone?

"Fan out. Find these people," the sheriff shouted in distress.

At that moment, Patrick came running up to the confused and bewildered Bob Parker. "He's gone!" He shouted out of breath. "He just disappeared! Jonathon was there one moment, and he just disappeared! Honest, I didn't take my eyes off him for a moment! He never even came to! He's just… gone!"

Stooping down to pick a discarded Bible up from off the ground, Bob numbly flipped the pages. A single piece of paper fell onto the ground from between its pages. Picking it up, he read the child-like handwriting out loud, "We must tell others about Jesus. He is coming back soon to take us all away in the Rapture. It will happen in the twinkling of an eye. We'll be here, then we'll be gone." He let his hand drop to his side. "The *Rapture*," he repeated quietly. "… What a ridiculous notion."

"For yourselves know perfectly
that the day of the LORD so
cometh as a theif in the night."
~~I Thessalonians 5:2

Meet the Author

Nishoni L. Harvey is a saved, sanctified, and soul-winning Baptist. Her husband, Matthew Harvey, and their three young children serve faithfully at Hope Baptist Church in Harrison, Michigan, where they are active members. A graduate of Landmark Baptist College, Nishoni loves teaching, writing stories and poetry, playing her instruments, and being a Mommy.

Nishoni's love for writing started as a young child, at which time she wrote imaginative stories that kept her family in suspense and eager for each new chapter to be completed so they could know what happened next in each tale. She went on to write for the "Blacksburg Times", a newspaper, as a teenager. She further culminated her writing skills by taking a course through the "Institute of Children's Literature" and by gaining her Bachelors in Secondary Education with a major in English. She continues to write often and is always in search of ways to use her talents for GOD.

MADE FOR MORE

30 DEVOTIONS TO HELP YOU
Overcome Challenges & Disappointment,
Confidently Step Into Your Purpose,
and Achieve Godly Success

Radhika Cruz

Made for More